JEFF NEWMAN

THE GREEDY WORM

Simon & Schuster Books for Young Readers
New York   London   Toronto   Sydney   New Delhi

SIMON & SCHUSTER BOOKS FOR YOUNG READERS • An imprint of Simon & Schuster Children's Publishing Division • 1230 Avenue of the Americas, New York, New York 10020 • © 2023 by Jeff Newman • Book design by Tom Daly © 2023 by Simon & Schuster, Inc. • All rights reserved, including the right of reproduction in whole or in part in any form. • SIMON & SCHUSTER BOOKS FOR YOUNG READERS and related marks are trademarks of Simon & Schuster, Inc. • For information about special discounts for bulk purchases, please contact Simon & Schuster Special Sales at 1-866-506-1949 or business@simonandschuster.com. • The Simon & Schuster Speakers Bureau can bring authors to your live event. For more information or to book an event contact the Simon & Schuster Speakers Bureau at 1-866-248-3049 or visit our website at www.simonspeakers.com. • The text for this book was set in Butterfly Ball. • The illustrations for this book were rendered digitally. • Manufactured in China • 1022 SCP • First Edition • 2 4 6 8 10 9 7 5 3 1 • Library of Congress Cataloging-in-Publication Data • Names: Newman, Jeff, 1976- author, illustrator. • Title: The greedy worm / Jeff Newman. • Description: First edition. | New York : Simon & Schuster Books for Young Readers, [2023] | Audience: Ages 4-8. | Audience: Grades k-1. | Summary: "One greedy worm has his eye on a very big apple and he doesn't want to share with any of the other hungry bugs. But when a bird starts eyeing the greedy worm, he learns the importance of sharing with friends"— Provided by publisher. • Identifiers: LCCN 2021039230 (print) | LCCN 2021039231 (ebook) | ISBN 9781442471955 (hardcover) | ISBN 9781442471986 (ebook) • Subjects: CYAC: Sharing–Fiction. | Worms–Fiction. | LCGFT: Picture books. • Classification: LCC PZ7.N47984 Gr 2023 (print) | LCC PZ7.N47984 (ebook) | DDC [E]–dc23 • LC record available at https://lccn.loc.gov/2021039230 • LC ebook record available at https://lccn.loc.gov/2021039231

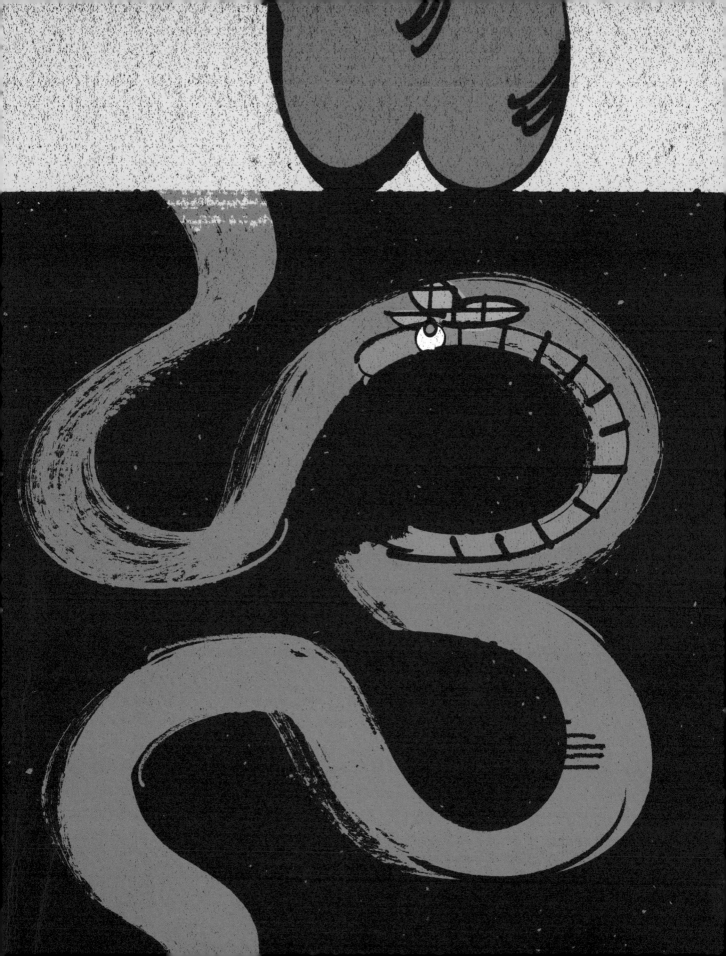

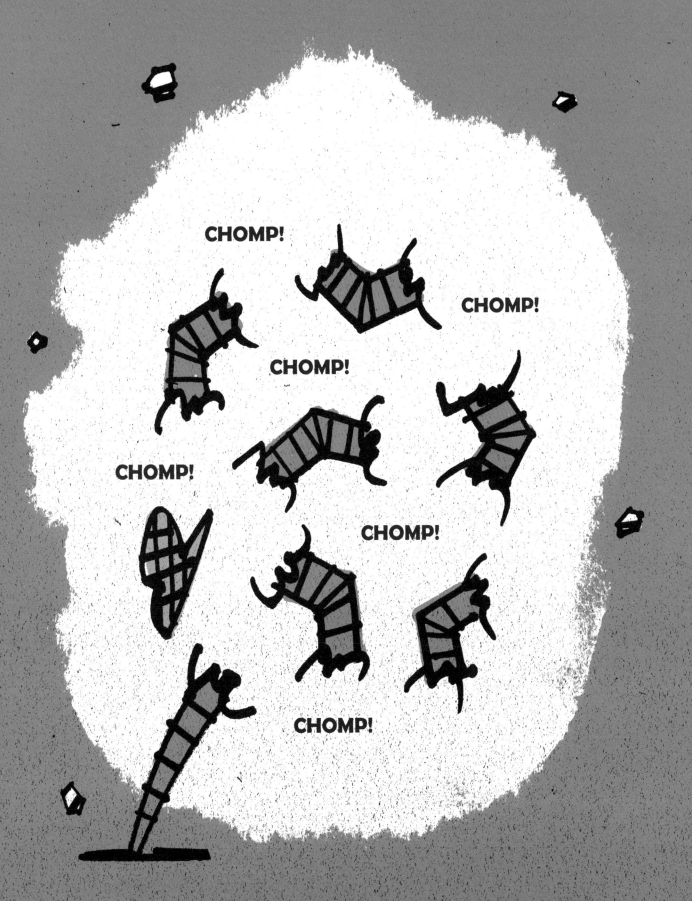

CRUNCH.